For Catherine and Joyce, with love — C. M-S. and G. S.

For Finn — J. B.

VIKING
Published by Penguin Group
Penguin Young Readers Group, 345 Hudson Street,
New York, New York 10014, U.S.A.
Penguin Group (Canada), 90 Eglinton Avenue East, Suite 700, Toronto, Ontario, Canada M4P 2Y3
(a division of Pearson Penguin Canada Inc.)
Penguin Books Ltd, 80 Strand, London WC2R 0RL, England
Penguin Ireland, 25 St Stephen's Green, Dublin 2, Ireland (a division of Penguin Books Ltd)
Penguin Group (Australia), 250 Camberwell Road, Camberwell, Victoria 3124, Australia
(a division of Pearson Australia Group Pty Ltd)
Penguin Books India Pvt Ltd, 11 Community Centre, Panchsheel Park, New Delhi – 110 017, India
Penguin Group (NZ), Cnr Airborne and Rosedale Roads, Albany, Auckland 1310, New Zealand
(a division of Pearson New Zealand Ltd)
Penguin Books (South Africa) (Pty) Ltd, 24 Sturdee Avenue, Rosebank, Johannesburg 2196, South Africa

Penguin Books Ltd, Registered Offices: 80 Strand, London WC2R 0RL, England

First published in Great Britain in 2006 by Puffin Books
First published in the United States in 2006 by Viking, a division of Penguin Young Readers Group

1   3   5   7   9   10   8   6   4   2

Text copyright © Christine Morton-Shaw and Greg Shaw, 2006
Illustrations copyright © John Butler, 2006

LIBRARY OF CONGRESS CATALOGING-IN-PUBLICATION DATA IS AVAILABLE
Viking ISBN 0-670-06175-1

Manufactured in China
Set in P22 Garamouche, Regular

Wake up, Sleepy Bear!

by Christine Morton-Shaw and Greg Shaw

illustrated by John Butler

VIKING

Hiding in the forest deep,
Friendly creatures, all asleep.
Today's a day to celebrate,
So wake up, wake up,
Don't be late!

Wake up, wake up, sleepy bear!
Time to rise, time to shine.
Hurry up, it's party time!

Stretch your paws out, scratch your back,
Rub your little eyes so black.
Snuffle-scuffle, find some honey,
Sticky-gold and yummy-runny.

Wake up, wake up, sleepy squirrels!

Time to rise, time to shine, hurry up, it's party time!

Help each other comb your tails,
Shine your little tiny nails.

Skitter-scatter, nuts to find,
Crunchy nuts of every kind!

Wake up, wake up, sleepy rabbits!
Time to rise, time to shine,
Hurry up, it's party time!

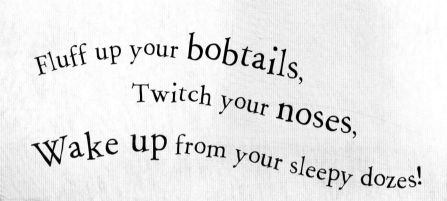

Fluff up your **bobtails**,
Twitch your **noses**,
Wake up from your sleepy dozes!

Sniffle-snuffle, roots to find,
Juicy roots of **every kind!**

Wake up, wake up, sleepy birds!

Time to rise, time to shine, hurry up, it's party time!

Preen your **feathers**, stretch your **wings**,

Shine your **beaks**, no time to sing!

Flitty-flappy, seeds to pick,
Scrunchy seeds, you must be **quick!**

Wake up, wake up, sleepy mice!

Time to rise, time to shine, hurry up, it's party time!

Wash your whiskers, leave your beds.
Get a move on, sleepyheads!

Scritchy-scratchy, find some berries,
Bright as jewels and red as cherries.

They're all awake, it's time to go.
See them creeping in a row
All along the forest floor.
The forest now is dark and deep.
Holding hands they quietly creep.
What is it they're looking for?

The creatures gather, all together,
Tiptoe nearer, fur and feather.

Softly, softly, smiles all round.
A little clearing they have found.
A cozy den within the trees,
A mother deer, on her knees . . .

. . . and such a tiny velvet snout!
Two twitchy ears, poking out,
Two big bright eyes, soft as feathers,
Four little legs, all twined together!

A little sigh, a little yawn,
A little, tiny,
brand-new fawn!

Wake up, wake up, sleepy fawn!
Time to rise, time to shine,
Time to start your living-time!

Welcome to our forest glen.
Hello, hello, hello again!

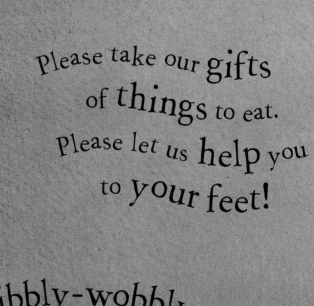

Please take our gifts
of things to eat.
Please let us help you
to your feet!

Wibbly-wobbly, legs uncurled . . .

Welcome to your brand-new world!